TILLY...A DEER'S TALE

(Based on a True Story)

Written by
Lee Manning-Vogelstein
Elizabeth Walker
Kristin Currid

Illustrated by
Chris Seale

Stone Hill Publishing
New York, NY

Copyright 2005

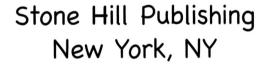

Copyright © by Lee Manning-Vogelstein
All rights reserved. No part of this book may be reproduced
in any form without written permission from the publisher.

Library of Congress CIP data on file.
ISBN 0-9765357-0-X
Text copyright ©2005 Lee Manning-Vogelstein
Illustration Copyright ©2005 Lee Manning-Vogelstein

Summary: Tilly, a whitetail deer, is rescued and rehabilitated.
Meet Tilly's new farm friends in a unique setting.

Published in the United States by
Stone Hill Publishing
New York, NY in 2005.

Printed and bound in South Korea.

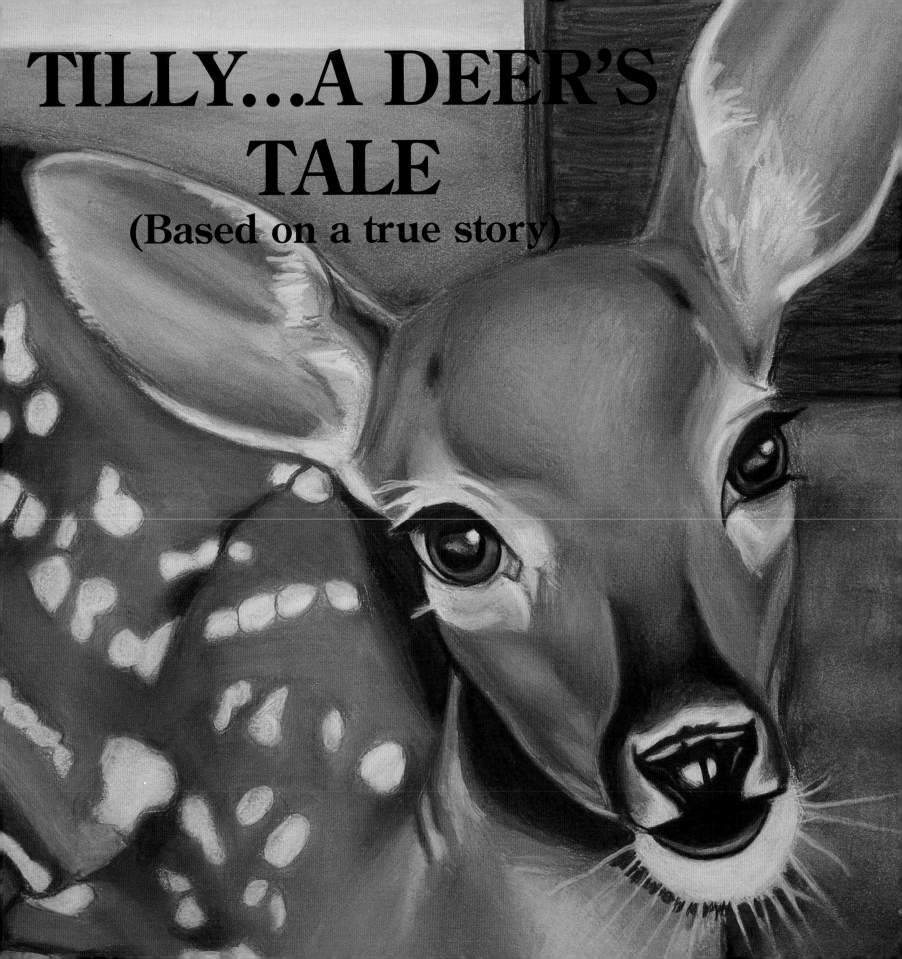

TILLY...A DEER'S TALE

(Based on a true story)

Dedications

For Dakota and Autumn Rose,
    My special grandchildren-L.M.V.

For my children,
    Kimberly, Corby and Jason-L.W.

For my Parents,
    Bill and Mimi Anderson-K.C.

Acknowledgments

For her generous artistic talent and invaluable attention to detail, thank you Kimberly Walker, Art Consultant.

For her compassionate, kind heart and inability to say no to any animal that needs to be rescued, it is a privilege to work with you Mary Schinittert, Licensed Wildlife Rehabilitator.

For her generous assistance and perseverance, thank you Sun Jackie Huh.

For her professional advice, encouragement and friendship, thank you Shannon Wilkinson.

This book is dedicated to the memory of Princess
who captured our hearts.

Dr. John Wilson has been practicing veterinary medicine for the past 33 years. Included among the numerous species, besides dogs and cats, he cares for are whitetail deer, fox, coyote, hawks, bald eagles, hedgehogs, turtles, squirrels of all kinds, horses, geese, ducks, swans and as you would expect, all farm animals.

Dr. Wilson's accomplishments have earned him the Green Chimneys Wildlife Award; a special tribute for the benefit of wildlife from the New York State Humane Association; a Certificate of Appreciation from the N.Y.S. Dept. of Environmental Conservation as well as recognition from the Hudson Valley Veterinary Medical Society for his extraordinary efforts to provide care to the wildlife population in N.Y. State.

Dr. Wilson is a graduate of New York State College of Veterinary Medicine University at Cornell University. He is diplomat of the American Board of Veterinary Practitioners, Certified in Canine and Feline Practice.

Dr. Wilson was born in Queens, NY. He worked as a young man at Claremont Riding Academy in N.Y.C. which his father once managed and was a part owner.

Dr. Wilson presently lives in Westchester, N.Y. with his wife, Tobé.

A Special Dedication

To

Dr. John A. Wilson

Dr. John (Jack) Wilson has been an
advisor, mentor and friend to us as
well as all the various animals that
are fortunate to be in his care.

With admiration

Lee, Lisa and Kristin
Princess and Tilly

What makes "Tilly...a Deer's Tale" so special? It is a story of people, animals and a collection of incidents that are mainly true. All people and animals mentioned by name really do exist.

It has been a privilege for Lisa, Kris, and me to work with the rescue deer. We never intended to become so involved, but once we took in Princess, we were all committed. She was the first and she was very special.

Our rescue deer arrive at our farm from many different sources. Neighbors, policemen, veterinarians and motorists, all bring orphaned deer to us. Many are only a few days old. We feed them, care for them and when they are ready, they are released back into the wild.

But, that is only the beginning. Many do not want to leave. They return to our farm and provide us with the most delightful memories, which we are happy to share with you, our readers. It is these antics that inspired us to write our story about Tilly and her friends. The specific nature of the events depicted in the book is true. We may have amalgamated some of the deer antics, as many deer have been rescued by us over the past six years and we had to simplify the storyline.

The illustrations that are so skillfully drawn by Chris Seale are impeccable and are most authentic. Our art consultant, Kimberly Walker, was scrupulous in making sure that the animal drawings were as representative of each animal as they could be. She certainly was successful.

After numerous drafts, our book was now complete, but we needed a title. We considered various options and then "Tilly...a Deer's Tale", suggested by our friend, Link Cross, was perfect. Our heartfelt thanks to Link.

We hope you will be as entertained in reading "Tilly" as we were in writing about her.

Lee Manning-Vogelstein

CHAPTERS

Tilly

Big Ben

Hazelnut

Wizzard

Jacques & Pierre

Holly

Mindy

Hershey

Photos by Christian Harder

ANIMALS

Carter

Tilt

Seymour Buns

Bucky

Buster

Beezie

Kit

Helen

J. Tottenham

14

Tilly lost her mother when she was very small.

Then she came to live here where she's loved by one and all.

She plays in the field with all of the others,

hide-and-go-seek with her sisters and brothers.

But Tilly is slightly different, you see.

The others have four perfect legs while Tilly has three.

No one seems to notice nor does Tilly seem to mind.

When she plays with all the others, she never lags behind.

Her courage and kindness are all that they see.

This is the story of our brave Miss Tilly!

All poems written by Mimi Anderson

Johnny goes fishing, his favorite love.
"Send me a big one!" he calls up above.
When what to his wondering eyes should appear,
floating downstream, but a scared baby deer.
Johnny jumps in to rescue the deer.
"Well little lady, I can't leave you here.
I know of a place that will care for you now,
loaded with lambs, goats and even a cow.
Friends, who will welcome you, keep you from harm.
I'm taking you home to the friendliest farm."

Krissy looks into the stall. "What's that?" Asks the baby deer as she looks up.

But, the fawn is so tired, she goes back to sleep in the nice soft blanket.

The farm is filled with many new sights and sounds.

Horses are neighing.

Chickens are clucking.

Ducks are quacking.

Pigs are oinking.

Sheep are bleating.

And Donkeys are braying.

"So many scary sounds!" exclaims the fawn.

"Where are they coming from?"

21

A big door opens and voices can be heard. Fisherman Johnny stops by to ask about the baby deer. "It's a good thing I was quick to catch her in my fishing net," says Johnny. "Yes, it was," Krissy replies, "You saved her. She's sleeping peacefully now."

The fawn can hear Fisherman Johnny's jeep as he heads out to fish on the river another day. It is going to be a busy morning at the farm for Krissy, and especially for the baby deer.

Krissy takes care of all the barnyard animals but she doesn't know what to feed a baby deer. In the wild, deer eat shrubs and berries, but this one is too young. She calls the veterinarian, Dr. Jack. Nurse Tobi promises the doctor will call her back very soon. While Krissy feeds hay and grain to the other animals in the barn, Dr. Jack calls. He tells her to feed goat's milk to the baby deer.

Whoops! The fawn tries to stand up, but her legs are weak. She starts to shiver and lies back down. "I'm very hungry," she says. "But what am I to eat?" Krissy pulls back the heavy door to the stall. "I guess you must be a very hungry little girl," she says, offering the fawn a baby bottle filled with goat's milk.

At first, the fawn is confused. "What is this?" she thinks. But, Krissy slips the nipple into her mouth and the fawn begins to drink. "This tastes good and I am so hungry," thinks the fawn. "Dr. Jack was right", says Krissy. "The fawn has finished all the goat's milk."

"I have work to do, but I'll be back" Krissy says.

"You have many new friends to meet in the barn."

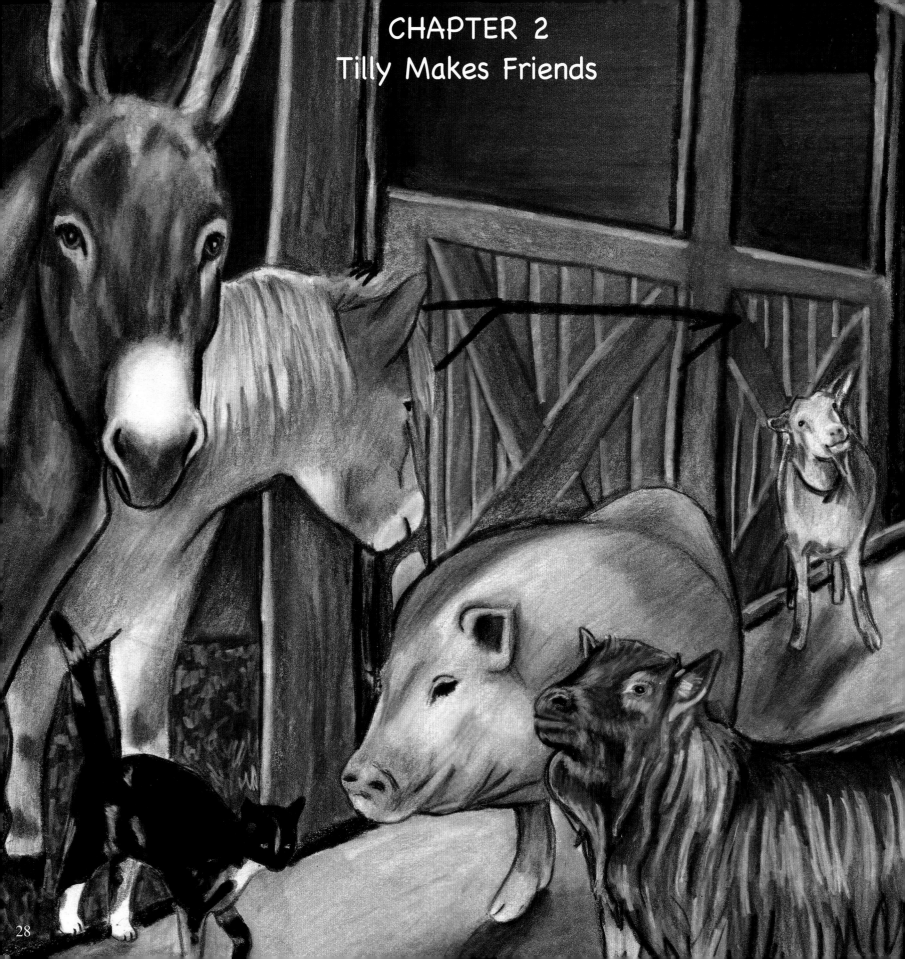

"We're most pleased to meet you,"
they said as a chorus;
the cats and the puppies,
the sheep and the horses.
The goats, ducks, and rabbits,
each gave a sweet smile.
"Looks like you're fixing
to stay for a while!"

Suddenly the fawn remembers how she tripped and became separated from her mother as they were walking beside the river, and how she began to float away. "I miss my mother," she says sadly.

Then Hershey and Holly, the farm's twin Labrador Retrievers, say hello to the fawn. She stares at them. "We are sorry you're lost," says Hershey. "And we are here to welcome you and show you the farm," adds Holly. Hershey and Holly, who are never apart and do everything together, take the fawn on her first tour of the farm.

"Well, who's this?" asks Big Ben the horse as he sees Hershey and Holly come down the aisle with a baby deer. "This is our new friend... wait, she doesn't have a name," says Holly. "I guess we will have to give her one then, won't we?" Says Big Ben. Big Ben has always named all the new animals that come to the farm. "She's as pretty as a filly with those long legs," Big Ben adds. "Yes, but she isn't a horse," says Holly. Big Ben thinks for a minute and says, "You're right. I name her....TILLY."

Just then Wizzard, the wise old goat, and Hazelnut, the cat, walk around the corner. "What's going on?" says Wizzard. "We have a new friend, Wizzard, and her name is Tilly," says Hershey. "Hello, Tilly, it's nice to meet you," says Wizzard. "Welcome to our farm," Hazelnut says, with a great big smile.

After Tilly meets all her new friends from the farm, her stomach begins to growl. "I'm hungry again," she says. "Let's all go to Krissy's house," replies Hershey. "She always has food out for us." "How will we get in?" asks Tilly. "Leave it to me," says Holly. Tilly watches in amazement as Holly presses down on the door handle and they all get in. "What a clever friend I have!" thinks Tilly.

"Thank you," she says.

"I was very hungry."

"We are happy to share our food,"

says Hershey.

Hershey and Holly curl up on their dog bed and get comfortable.

"Tilly", says Holly, "come share our bed". "I am so proud to have a name", thinks Tilly. It has been a long day. Krissy has just finished the evening feeding in the barn. When she opens the door, she is surprised. There, sleeping together are Hershey, Holly and Tilly — all new friends.

Look at the green fields – all the places to roam!
"Be careful," says Wizzard, "Don't stray far from home."
But there's so much to see and so much to explore.
And so many friends that I've come to adore.

Krissy is out in the field playing catch with Hershey and Holly.

"May I get the stick?" asks Tilly. "Sure," says Hershey.

"Let's see how fast you can run," adds Holly.

Tilly runs very fast. In fact, she runs faster than Hershey or Holly. She brings the stick to Krissy. "Tilly, you are very fast for such a little girl," says Krissy. Tilly can't wait to chase the stick again.

"Holly, what is all that noise?" asks Tilly. "It's the chicken house," replies Holly. "Follow me." Krissy, Hershey, Holly and Tilly all run to the chicken house. Carter, the fainting goat, is lying outside the chicken house. When they look inside, Helen the hen is upside down on the floor.

Tilly can't believe her eyes. Krissy turns Helen right side up.

"Helen sleeps upside down," explains Hershey.

"Nothing to get upset about!" "But what about the goat?" asks Tilly. "Oh, that's just Carter," Hershey says. "He forgets Helen is just sleeping and gets worried. When he worries, he faints." "Nothing to get upset about!" adds Holly.

Tilly thinks how funny it is, a hen that sleeps upside down and a goat that faints. "What other unusual animals live here?" she wonders. Tilly strolls up the path toward the farm pond with her friends.

Tilly and friends get to the pond and see Hazelnut, the cat, on the opposite side. "What are you doing?" asks Hershey. "I'm watching fish," Hazelnut replies. "Can I watch too?" asks Tilly. "Be careful," yells Holly. "You'll get all wet," adds Hershey. Too late. Tilly is so curious to see what Hazelnut is looking at, that she falls in the pond. "Brrrr, it's cold!" exclaims Tilly. As Tilly shakes off the water, Hazelnut gets soaking wet, then scampers back to the barn.

The others follow, leaving Tilly alone to explore the woods.

CHAPTER 4
Tilly and the Stone Wall

I know that Wizzard said not to stray far,
there are things that can harm me,
I think he said "car".
But it's sunny and warm, and I want to jump high,
over the fences and up to the sky.

While Tilly is out exploring, she sees a road. She has heard about roads and the cars that drive on them from the other animals on the farm. Wizzard, the wise old goat, told all the young animals to be very careful of the cars. "Cars are dangerous," he warned, "and animals can get hurt."

Whoops! Too late...a car sees Tilly and honks it's horn. She jumps over a stone wall to keep from being hit. "Ouch!" Her leg hurts terribly when she lands. Tilly's leg is broken. Confused and lost, Tilly realizes she doesn't know how to get back home.

After what seems like a very long time, Tilly hears someone calling.
"Tilly, Tilly," shouts the voice. "Over here!" Tilly replies.
It is Hazelnut the cat. "All the animals at the farm are worried,
so I came looking for you," she says.

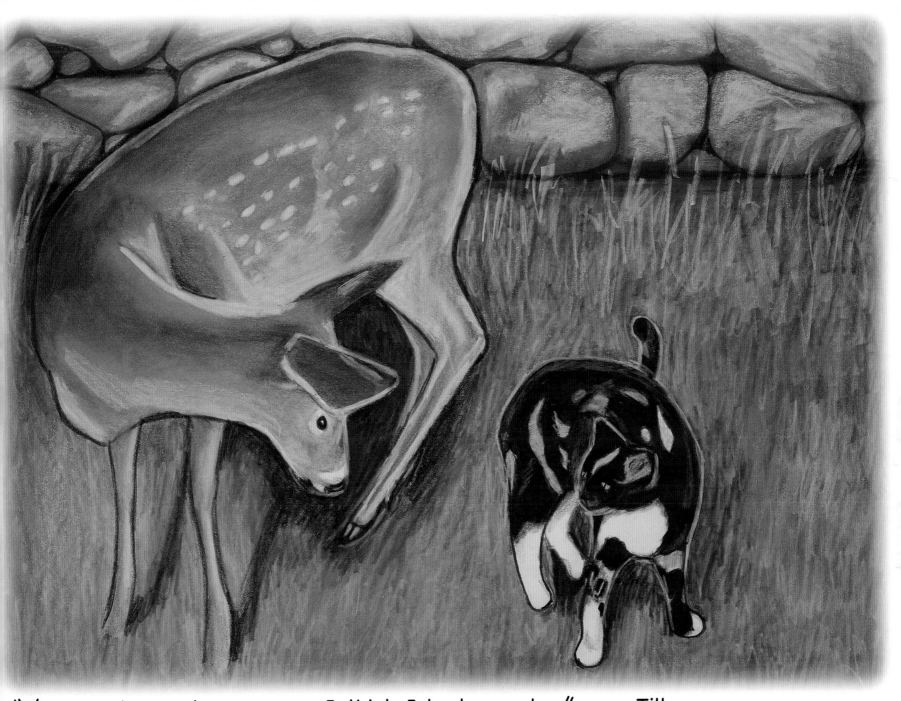

"I'm very happy to see you. I think I broke my leg," says Tilly.

"I can't walk." "Sure, you can," says Hazelnut. "Do just like me." Hazelnut

begins to walk holding up one leg and walking on three legs. "Do you think I

can?" asks Tilly. "Sure, you can," replies Hazelnut. "Let's go back to the farm.

Krissy will know how to help you."

Tilly copies Hazelnut and walks on three legs. It is hard. But after a few tries, she manages to walk slowly. They walk most of the day. From time to time, Tilly has to stop and rest.

It is very late when Tilly and Hazelnut reach the farm. The other animals see Tilly enter the barn. They start talking and asking each other questions. Hazelnut leads Tilly into her stall where there is lots of fresh straw upon which she can rest. "Don't worry, Tilly" says Hazelnut. "I'll stay with you. Holly and Hershey have gone to get Krissy."

Hazelnut, kitty cat, kisses my cheek.

Even the bunnies decide to speak.

The sheep and the goats and even the chicks,

say, "Get better, Tilly. Please don't be sick."

With such friends and family, it's easy to tell,

that sooner than later, I know I'll get well.

"Is that you Holly?" asks Krissy as she hears the door open. Holly and Hershey are barking and running back and forth from the kitchen to the door. Holly opens the door and runs back out to the barn. Krissy says, "Hershey, what's the matter? Let's follow Holly and find out what the problem could be." Hershey leads the way. "I'll take Krissy right to Tilly's stall," thinks Hershey.

"Tilly, what's happened?" asks Krissy. "Are you okay?" Krissy approaches Tilly.
"Stand up, Tilly." "Go ahead," says Hazelnut. "Let Krissy see your leg."
Tilly tries to stand up, but she falls down.

"This is serious. I must call Dr. Jack," thinks Krissy. "You rest right here, I'll be
back soon. Hershey and Holly will stay with you." Hazelnut curls up next to Tilly
to keep her warm while Krissy runs to call the doctor.

"Thank you, Hazelnut, for staying with me," says Tilly as Hazelnut grooms her. "You are my best friend," replies Hazelnut. "I'll always be here to help you." Carter comes wondering into the stall, sees Tilly and faints. All this is too upsetting for him. "Not again!" cries Mindy the lamb, looking down at him. "What are we to do with you?" The chickens perch on Carter's back for a better view.

"Let's not worry about Carter", says Wizzard, "He always wakes up."
"It's Tilly we need to worry about. I warned her about those cars."
"It was right of you to warn her, but the young ones always want to explore and see for themselves," adds Big Ben the horse. Wizzard and Big Ben consider Tilly's future life in the woods, as a wild deer.

"How will she take care of herself with a broken leg?"
Worries Big Ben.

Hazelnut wishes she could go with Tilly to Dr. Jack's so Tilly won't be scared.

"Be brave," Hazelnut says. "I'll be here when you return!"

Helen and the bunnies, Seymour Buns and Tilt, watch as Krissy drives away to Dr. Jack's. "I hope she doesn't have to stay overnight at Dr. Jack's," says Big Ben. Wizzard agrees. "She won't know anyone there. That can be scary for a fawn."

Jacques and Pierre, the French donkeys, have cantered up from the lower field.

"*Vhat ees going on ere?*" Asks Jacques. "*Yew all luk suuu sad.*" "Krissy took the young deer to Dr. Jack's," explains Big Ben. "The fawn broke her leg."

"*Weel Dr. Jack poot a cast on er leg?*" asks Pierre. "I hope not," says Helen. "How can she walk with a cast?" "Yes, how can she run and jump?" asks Tilt. They are all very worried about Tilly.

"Well, Krissy, she's a lucky fawn," says Dr. Jack. "The leg's broken, but the problem could have been even more serious. I'll wrap it up, but it could take months to heal," the doctor adds. "I suspect she will have a limp." Nurse Tobi, who is holding the fawn, remarks how pretty she is. "She's lucky to have you taking care of her on such a wonderful farm," she says to Krissy. "Call me if you have any problems."

"Good-bye and thank you," Krissy replies.
She drives back to the farm and the waiting animals.

The fawn is happy to be home in her stall with all her friends, but especially Hazelnut. "Good to have you back" remarks Big Ben. "You will have to be more careful in the woods." "Yes, I will," says Tilly. Tilly is so tired from her eventful day that she falls right to sleep with Hazelnut by her side.

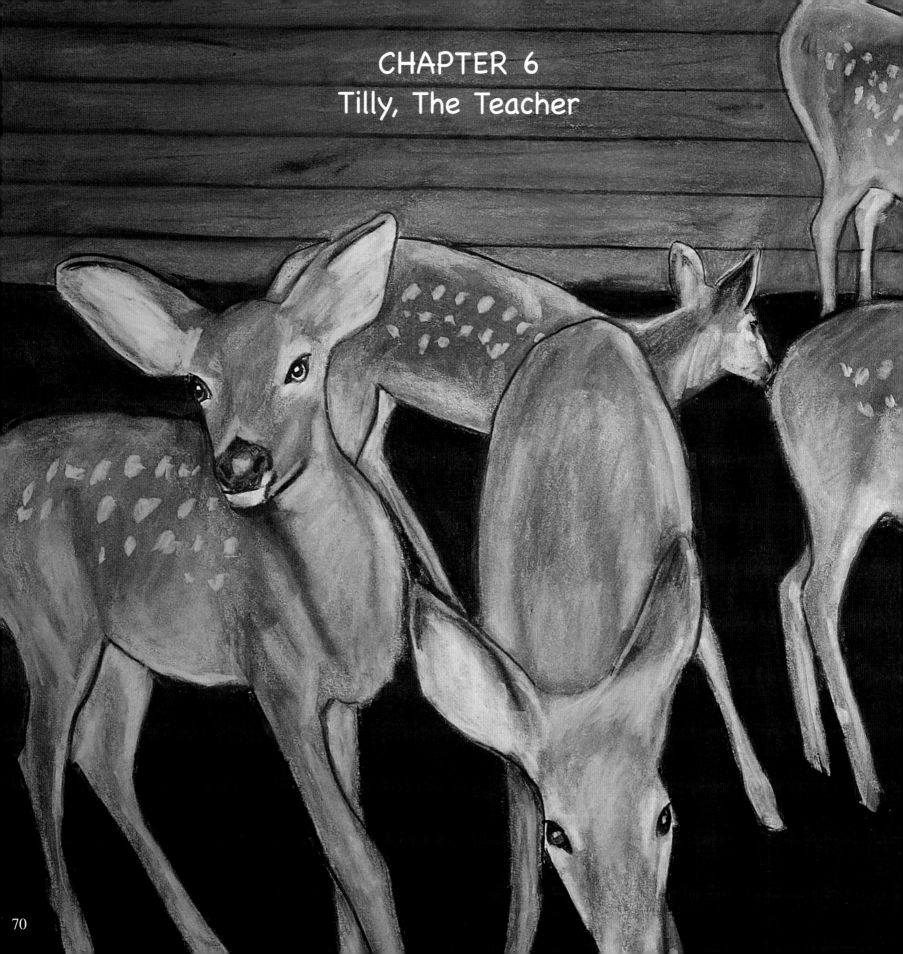

I see now a teacher is what I'll become.

I'll teach all these fawns how to jump and to run.

I'll think up their names and make sure that they fit:

We'll have Bucky and Buster and Beezie and Kit.

"Hazelnut, I don't think I'll ever walk right again", says Tilly. "Yes, you will," she replies. "I limp, and what about running and jumping?" says Tilly. "I've seen you do all that," says Hazelnut. "Dr. Jack said it would take months for your leg to heal, but you will feel stronger everyday." Hazelnut encourages.

In the months to come Tilly is running and playing with all her friends on the farm. Her limp is still there but it doesn't keep her from having fun.

"*Mindy ese having luts of foon with Holly and Hershey, loook at theem run,*" says
Jacques. "Quick, quick," says Mindy, "come outside, it's the first snow." Tilly
is very confused, she looks outside and everything is white. "Oh, no," says Tilly,
"what is all the white stuff out there?" "*She's nev-air seen snew before,*" says
Pierre.

"Come on, let's go," says Seymour Buns as he jumps out into the snow and disappears. This is so much fun. Everything is so white and it looks like a winter wonderland. "I hope it never stops snowing," thinks Tilly.

All the fields are green again and spring has arrived. The days are longer and warmer. "Hi Tilly, Hi Wizzard," Krissy calls out. "Want to come and meet the new baby deer. Dr. Jack just brought them to us. I think they may be twins." Krissy adds. "Twins?" says Tilly. "What are we supposed to do with twins?" "Let's go say hello. Perhaps they were lost from their mother, as you were, Tilly," remarks Wizzard.

"Is it true? Are you twins?" asks Tilly. "Yes, we're brothers," replies one.

"Why are you here?" asks Tilly. "We think our mother got lost.

A family found us while they were hiking and took us to Dr. Jack," said the

other baby deer. "But, what will we do here?" asked his brother. "Krissy will

take care of you," replied Hazelnut. "And I can help, too," adds Tilly.

Ben decides to name the new fawns Bucky and Buster. As Krissy gives them their first bottles of goat's milk, Dr. Jack arrives with two more fawns.

"That makes four fawns. I'm going to be very busy," thought Tilly. "We have to make sure they eat properly and stay healthy. Next year, when they are ready, they will be set free. Until that time, I'm going to have to teach them all about living in the woods," Tilly says.

Tilly knows she has an important job to do. "Don't forget to warn them about the cars," says Wizzard. "I won't," replies Tilly. She will help Bucky and Buster and the two new fawns they named, Beezie and Kit, to be careful when they are alone in the woods.

Big Ben smiles to himself as he remembers how they all first welcomed Tilly to the farm. He knows that the new fawns will be taught well by Tilly. Big Ben is very pleased that Tilly is happy as a teacher and has found her place on the farm.

Please visit Tilly at our website:
Tillyadeerstale.com

Join Tilly and her friends and watch her discover
the many delightful antics of growing up on the farm.

A variety of "Tilly" merchandise is available for sale
to further enhance your child's amusement and affection
for all the characters in the Tilly story.

A portion of the proceeds from the sale of "Tilly" merchandise
will be donated to animal rescue organizations.

To make a donation directly to any of these organizations,
a list is available on the website.